CLEVER GRETCHEN

AND OTHER FORGOTTEN FOLKTALES

Retold by
Alison Lurie

CLEVER
GRETCHEN
AND OTHER FORGOTTEN
FOLKTALES

Illustrated by
Margot Tomes

THOMAS Y. CROWELL
New York

Several of the stories in this book first appeared in *Horizon* Magazine.

Designed by Kohar Alexanian

LC-78-22512

Trade ISBN 0-690-03943-3   Library ISBN 0-690-03944-1
4 5 6 7 8 9 10

For Rebecca, Clarissa, and Amanda Cooke

CONTENTS

ACKNOWLEDGMENTS

I should like to thank Charles McLaughlin of *Horizon* magazine, who first suggested this project to me; also my students in children's literature at Cornell University, whose lively interest in folktales encouraged me to expand an article into a book. I am most grateful to Shelley Clauson and Sarah Liddington for editorial and secretarial assistance beyond the call of academic and professional duty—and, especially, to Diana Chlebek, without whose imaginative research and remarkable knowledge of European languages *Clever Gretchen* could not have been completed.

A.L.

INTRODUCTION

I N the fairy tales we know best today, the heroes seem to have all the interesting adventures. They get to kill dragons and outwit giants and rescue princesses and find the magic treasure. As for the heroines, things just happen to them: they are persecuted by wicked step-mothers, eaten by wolves, or fall asleep for a hundred years. All most of them ever seem to do is wait patiently for the right prince to come, or for someone else to rescue them from dangers and enchantments. This has made some people say that modern children ought not to read fairy tales, because they will get the idea that girls are supposed to be beautiful and good and helpless and dull.

But there are thousands of folktales in the world that are not at all like this. They have heroines who can fight and hunt as well as any man, heroines who defeat giants, answer riddles, outwit the Devil, and rescue their friends and relatives from all sorts of dangers and evil spells. They are not only beautiful and good, but also strong, brave, clever, and resourceful.

Why don't we know these stories as well as the others? It is because the first collections of fairy tales for children were put together over a hundred years ago, when women and girls were supposed to be weak and helpless; and the editors who picked the stories out of the many that were available chose ones like "Snow White," "Cinderella," "Sleeping Beauty," and "Little Red Riding-Hood." These tales were printed over and over again, while the rest were almost forgotten.

Most of the editors who chose these stories were men. The original tellers of folktales, on the other hand, were mainly women. And they were not frail Victorian ladies, but working women: farmers' wives, shopkeepers, craftswomen, household servants, children's nurses, and midwives. They lived active, interesting lives, and the stories they told show it.

I have tried to rescue some of their almost forgotten tales from among the many recorded by scholars during the last century in all the countries of Europe. Most of them were recorded many times, and often in many different countries. I have retold them freely in my own words, often putting together different versions of the

same story, but trying to preserve the spirit of the origi-
nals.

I hope that this book will help to end the ill favor
into which fairy tales have lately fallen—and even that,
one day, some of its heroines may be as well known as
Cinderella and Snow White are now.

CLEVER
GRETCHEN

ONCE upon a time there lived a lord who had a daughter named Gretchen, who was as clever as she was good, and pretty besides. Rich merchants and noblemen came from all over the country to ask her hand in marriage, but her father would have none of them. "The man who marries my daughter," said he, "must be the best huntsman in the world."

Now in the village nearby there was a poor widow's son called Hans, who got it into his head that he would like to marry Gretchen himself. "Alas, poor boy, that can never be," said his mother; for though Hans was a good-natured lad and she loved him dearly, yet he was a bit simple.

"A man can but try," said Hans. And he put his cap on his head and his gun over his shoulder and set out for the castle. Yet his mother's words rang in his head, and he trudged along sadly.

Now as he came to the crossroads, he met a tall stranger dressed all in red, with feet like a goat's. "Where are you going today, Hans, and why do you look so downhearted?" asked the stranger.

"I am going up to the castle to ask for Gretchen's hand in marriage," said Hans, who was surprised that the stranger knew his name. "But I doubt if she'll have me, for her father has promised to give her only to the best huntsman in the world."

"Why, that is nothing to be downhearted about," said the stranger. "If you will sign your name to this paper, I can make you the best huntsman in the world immediately."

And what did the paper say, Hans wanted to know. Oh, only that after seven years Hans would go away with the stranger and be his servant, unless Hans could ask him a question he could not answer.

"Very well," said Hans, for he thought that seven years was a long time, and he signed his name to the paper. The tall stranger took Hans's gun and blew down its barrel, and the thing was done.

So Hans went on up to the castle. "What do you want?" said the guard at the gate.

"I am the best huntsman in the world," said

Hans, "and I have come to marry Gretchen."

The guard only laughed at him, for he looked so simple, and told him to go away. Hans did not go away, however; he stood and waited by the gate. By and by Gretchen looked out and saw him standing there. When she heard what he had come for, she smiled, and told the guard to let him come in and speak to her father.

When Gretchen's father, the lord, saw Hans, he laughed also. "So you are the greatest huntsman in the world," he said.

"Yes," said Hans.

"Indeed," said the lord. "And could you shoot a feather out of the tail of that sparrow I see now flying over the castle tower?"

"A man can but try," said Hans, and he raised his gun to his shoulder. Bang! and down fell a feather onto the grass at their feet.

"Well done!" cried Gretchen.

"Yes," said the lord, frowning, for he did not want to give his daughter to a poor simpleton. "But could you shoot the tail off that hare I see now running across the meadow?"

Bang! and off went the hare's tail as neatly as if it were cut with a pair of shears.

"Well done!" cried Gretchen again.

"Yes," said the lord, frowning still harder. "But

could you shoot the pipe out of the mouth of my steward over on yonder hill where they are haying?" And he pointed away across the fields.

"Father, for shame," said Gretchen. "No huntsman living could shoot so far."

"Nay, let him try," said the lord; for he was determined to be rid of Hans.

Bang! went the gun. And presently all the haymakers came running back over the fields to the castle, crying that they could not go on with their work, for someone was shooting at them and had knocked the steward's pipe right out of his mouth.

Then the lord saw that he was beaten, and he thought besides that it would not be a bad thing to have a son-in-law who could shoot like that. So Hans and Gretchen were married, and lived together in joy.

Seven years is not such a long time after all when you are happy. When Hans saw that they had nearly gone by, he lost his good spirits and became sad and downhearted. Gretchen, his wife, noticed this, and asked what his trouble was. At first he would not say, but she begged and begged, and at last he told her how seven years ago he had met a tall stranger dressed in red, with feet like a goat's.

"That was the Evil One," said Gretchen.

If Hans was sad before, he was terrified now. He

told Gretchen how he had signed the paper, and that the very next day he must go away with the stranger and be his servant, unless he could ask a question the Evil One could not answer.

Gretchen said to Hans that he must keep up his courage, and perhaps she could help him. She thought for a while, and then said that tomorrow she would do thus and so, and he should say this and that, and between them they might defeat the Evil One after all.

So the next morning Gretchen took off her clothes and smeared herself all over with honey. Then she ripped open her bed pillows and rolled herself in feathers.

Presently the stranger came up the road to the castle, and there was Hans waiting for him at the gate with his gun.

"Are you ready to go with me, Hans?" said the stranger, smiling.

Yes, Hans said, he was ready; only he wanted to ask one favor. Might he have a last shot with his gun before they went?

"Very well," said the stranger; and they set off together over the fields.

By and by they saw a sparrow. "Shoot at that," said the stranger.

"Oh, no," said Hans. "A sparrow is too small."

So they went on a little farther, and by and by they saw a hare. "Shoot at that," said the stranger.

"Oh, no," said Hans. "A hare is too small, and too low down."

So they went on a little farther. By and by they came to a plowed field, and there was something skipping and hopping across the furrows that looked like a great bird. It was Gretchen, with honey and feathers stuck all over her. "Shoot at that; shoot at that!" cried the stranger.

"Oh, yes," said Hans. "I will shoot at that." He raised his gun to his shoulder and took aim. Then he lowered it again. "But what is it?" said he.

The stranger looked at Gretchen, but he could not tell what she was. "Never mind about that," he said. "Shoot, for we must be going."

"Very well," said Hans. "But what is it?"

The stranger screwed up his eyes and looked again, but he knew no more than before. "Never mind about that," he said. "Shoot and be done with it, for they are waiting for us at home."

"Yes, certainly," said Hans. "But what is it?"

"Hell and damnation!" cried the stranger. "I do not know what it is."

"Then be off with you," said Hans, "for you could not answer my question."

The stranger snorted like a goat, and stamped the

ground, and fled away over the fields and hills.

As for Hans and Gretchen, they went home to-gether, and lived in joy ever after.

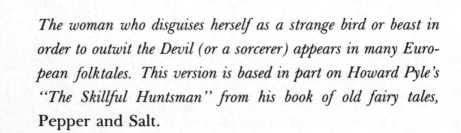

The woman who disguises herself as a strange bird or beast in order to outwit the Devil (or a sorcerer) appears in many Euro-pean folktales. This version is based in part on Howard Pyle's "The Skillful Huntsman" from his book of old fairy tales, Pepper and Salt.

MANKA
AND THE
JUDGE

ONCE there were two peas-
ants, one well-off and
one poor. They were digging together in a field, and as
they turned over the earth they found a cup made of
gold. "It is mine!" shouted one, "for I saw it first."
"No," cried the other, "it is mine, for I pulled it out of
the ground!" At last they agreed to go before the judge
and let him decide the matter.

Now the judge in the village was young and had not
been long in his post, and he was puzzled by the case.
So he said to the peasants that he would ask them three
riddles, and whoever could give him the right answers
within three days should have the cup. And the riddles
were: "What is the richest thing in the world? What is the
heaviest thing in the world? What is the swiftest thing in
the world?"

The well-to-do peasant went home and told his wife

what the judge had said. "Oh, that's easy," cried she. "The richest thing in the world is the king; the heaviest is iron; and the swiftest is surely our bay mare, for she can outrun any horse in the country."

The poor peasant also went home to his cottage, where there was no one to greet him but his daughter Manka, for his wife was dead. For two days he puzzled over the riddles, sighing much and scratching his head. At last Manka asked him what was the matter. "The judge has set me three riddles," he answered, "and if I can answer them tomorrow, I will win the golden cup we found in the field. But for the life of me I cannot do it."

"And what are the riddles?" said Manka. So her father repeated them to her.

"Go to the judge tomorrow" Manka said, "and tell him that the richest thing is the earth, because she brings forth all that we need in this world; that the heaviest thing is sorrow, which lies on mankind with a greater weight than iron; and that the swiftest thing is the mind, for it can go to China and back in a moment."

The next day the two peasants appeared again before the judge. He heard their answers, and awarded the golden cup to the poor man. "Tell me," he said. "Did you solve my riddles by yourself, or did someone help you?"

"Your honor," replied the peasant, "I have a daughter called Manka, who is very wise for her years, and she told me what to say."

"I should like to see this Manka," said the judge. "Pray bring her here tomorrow."

When Manka and her father appeared in court next day, they saw two brothers there who had come to settle a quarrel. Their father had left them a farm, of which part was good rich land and the rest barren, and they could not agree between them how to share it. Whichever one divided the property, the other was dissatisfied; and when the judge tried to divide it, both were dissatisfied. "Since you are so wise, Manka," said the young judge, "tell me what to do in this case."

"Very well," said Manka. "Let one brother divide the farm, and let the other take first choice." And so it was done, and the men went away content.

The judge looked again at Manka, and saw that she was as pretty as she was clever. "I should like to marry your daughter," he said to her father. Manka was willing, and so it was arranged. But when the judge's family heard of it they protested, saying that Manka was only a poor peasant girl, and not good enough for him. So at last the judge sent word to Manka that he would marry her on a certain day, but only if she would come to him neither clothed nor naked, neither walking nor riding, and neither with a wedding gift nor without one.

"Alas, Manka," said her father when he heard this. "I fear you will never be wed."

"Do not worry," said his daughter, "but go to market and buy a fishing net and a live pigeon."

Her father shook his head, but he did as she had said. As soon as he returned, Manka took off her clothes and wrapped herself in the net, so that she was neither clothed nor naked. Then she saddled the old billy goat, mounted him, put the pigeon under her arm, and set off for the court. As she went, her feet dragged on the ground, so that she was neither walking nor riding.

When the judge came out to meet her, Manka handed him the pigeon, saying, "Here is your wedding gift." But as he touched it, the bird shook its wings and flew away. The judge laughed, took Manka by the hand, and said, "You have done as I asked, and now we shall be married. Only one thing you must promise me: that you will never interfere with my judgments in court."

So Manka and the judge were wed, and for a time they lived together well enough. One day, however, two peasants came into court. They had been hauling goods to market, and a mare belonging to one of them had lain down under the other's cart and given birth to a foal. Both men claimed the foal as theirs. The judge heard the

case, and decided in favor of the man who owned the cart, saying, "Where the beast was born, there let it remain."

Now the peasant who had lost the case had heard that the judge's wife was both wise and kindhearted, so he went to her and told the whole story. At first Manka did not want to help him, because of her promise, but he wept so that at last she said, "If you will swear not to give me away, I'll tell you what to do. Tomorrow morning take a pail of water and a fishing rod, stand in the road where my husband will pass, and drop your line in as if you were fishing." And she also told him what to say to the judge.

Next day, when the judge was on his way to court, he saw the peasant standing in the road. "What are you doing there?" he asked.

"Fishing," said the man.

"But, you poor fool, you can't catch fish in a pail of water," said the judge.

"There's just as much chance of my catching fish in a pail as there is of a cart giving birth to a foal."

The judge smiled, and then frowned. "You are right," he said, "and I was wrong. You may take back your foal. But first, you must tell me who it was that taught you how to answer me."

For a while the man swore that no one had aided him, but at last he confessed that it was His Honor's own wife who had told him what to say. "I thought so," said the judge. He went home and said angrily to Manka, "You have broken your promise, and I cannot live with you any longer. You must go back to your father."

"Very well, if that is your wish," said Manka. "I will go this evening after supper; only give me leave to take with me whatever I love best in the house." "So be it," said the judge. "Take whatever you want." Manka threw her arms around him and kissed him, and they sat down to supper. But as they ate, she slipped a sleeping potion into his glass, and he had hardly finished when he fell into a heavy sleep.

When the judge was snoring, Manka called the servants and told them to set him in the carriage and drive with her to her father's house. There they put him to bed.

The judge slept all that night and part of the next day, and when he woke he did not know where he was. He called for his servants, but there were no servants there. Instead, Manka came running, and said to him, "Dear love, you are at home with me in my father's cottage. You told me I might take with me whatever in your house I loved best, and I have done so."

Her husband laughed, and said, "You are wiser than I. Let us go home, and from this day forth we shall sit in court and give judgment together." And so it was done.

This story is known throughout Europe—my version combines motifs from Russian and German tales. The riddles and their answers are very old, and the point made in them (and again at the end of the tale) is that human thoughts and feelings are more important than worldly goods.

THE
BLACK GEESE

L ONG ago there lived a man and wife who had two children, a girl and a boy. One day the woman said to her daughter, "Elena, we are going to market today; stay in the house while we are away, and look after your baby brother, for Baba Yaga's black geese who steal children have been seen flying over the village. When we come home, we will bring you some sugar buns."

After her mother and father were gone, Elena stayed in the house with her brother for a little while. But soon she got tired of this, and took him outside to where her friends were playing. She put him down on the grass and joined in their games, and presently she forgot all about him and ran off. The black geese came down, seized the little boy, and carried him away.

When Elena came back and found her brother gone, she was very frightened. She rushed to look in every corner of the house and yard, but could not see him. She shouted his name, but he did not answer. At last she said to herself that the black geese must have stolen her brother and taken him to Baba Yaga, the terrible witch of the forest, who is eight feet tall and eats little children. "I must go after him," Elena said. And she began to run toward the forest.

She ran across the fields and came to a pond, and there she saw a fish lying on the bank, gasping for water.

"Elena, Elena!" it called. "I am dying!"

Elena wanted to hurry on, but she was sorry for the fish. So she picked it up and put it carefully in the pond, where it sank and then rose again to the surface. "As you have helped me, so I shall help you," said the fish. "Here, take this shell. If ever you are in danger, throw it over your shoulder."

Elena did not see how a shell could help her, but she did not want to seem rude, so she put it in her pocket and ran on. Presently she came to a grove of trees, and there she saw a squirrel caught in a trap.

"Elena, Elena!" it called. "My leg is caught!" Elena wanted to go on, but she felt sorry for the squirrel. So she released the trap. The squirrel darted up into a tree, and down again. "As you have helped me, so I shall help you," it said. "Here, take this walnut. If ever you are in danger, throw it over your shoulder."

Elena put the nut in her pocket and hurried on. Soon she came to a stony bank, and there she saw a field mouse trying to move a fallen rock.

"Elena, Elena!" it called. "I cannot get into my hole!" Elena was sorry for the field mouse, so she pushed and shoved until she had moved the rock aside. The mouse darted into its hole, and reappeared. "As you have helped me, so I shall help you," it said. "Take this pebble. If ever you are in danger, throw it over your shoulder."

Elena put the pebble in her pocket, and ran on into the dark forest, where the trees grow so close together that not a speck of sunshine can get through them. Soon she came to a clearing, and there she saw Baba Yaga's hut, which stands on three giant hens' legs and can move about when it likes. The black geese were roosting on the roof of the hut, a kettle was boiling on the fire, and Baba Yaga was asleep inside, snoring through her long nose. Near her on the floor sat Elena's little brother, playing with some bones.

Elena crept into the hut and picked up her brother. But as she ran away into the forest, the black geese saw her. They began to honk and to clap their wings, and Baba Yaga woke up.

"Stop, thief!" she screamed. "Bring back my dinner!"

Elena did not stop, or answer the witch, but hurried on with her little brother in her arms; and Baba Yaga came out of her hut and started after them on her long bony legs.

Elena could not run very fast, because her brother was too heavy. When she came out of the forest and looked back, she saw that the witch was gaining on them. What could she do? Suddenly she remembered what the fish had said, so she reached into her pocket and threw the shell over her shoulder.

At once a broad lake appeared behind her. It was too large for Baba Yaga to go around it, so she squatted down by the edge and began to drink. She drank so fast that the water began to sink at once, and it was not long before she had drunk up the whole lake. Then she ran on.

Elena looked back, and saw that the lake was gone and that Baba Yaga was gaining on them again. She remembered what the squirrel had said, reached into her pocket, and threw the walnut over her shoulder.

At once a thick grove of trees sprang up behind her. They grew so close together that Baba Yaga could not get through. So she began to chew up the trees with her sharp teeth. She ate so fast that in a few minutes she had eaten up the whole grove of trees. Then she ran on.

Elena looked back again, and saw that the trees were

gone, and the witch was coming after her again, so close that she could hear her gnashing her long teeth and see her reaching out her bony arms to grab them. She felt in her pocket and threw the pebble over her shoulder.

Instantly a stony mountain sprang up behind her, so tall that its top was lost in clouds. Baba Yaga could not eat it or drink it; and she could not get over it. So she had to go back into the forest, growling and cursing.

As for Elena, she went on to her village, and was safe at home playing with her little brother when her father and mother got back from market with the sugar buns.

The dreaded Russian witch, Baba Yaga, who appears in this story and many others, usually travels in a mortar, steering it with a pestle and sweeping away her tracks with a broom.

MIZILCA

Long ago and far away, there lived a knight who was skilled in magic. One day a messenger came to him from the Sultan, demanding that the knight come with horse and arms, or send one of his sons, to serve the Sultan for a year and a day. The knight did not know what to do, for he was old and lame, and had no sons, only three daughters. So troubled was he that he ceased to take any joy in living. At home and abroad he was continually downcast, and whenever he looked at his children he would sigh and shake his head.

At last his eldest daughter, whose name was Stanuta, said to him, "Dear father, what ails you? Have we done something to displease you?"

"No, my child," said the knight. "I am sighing because the Sultan has commanded me to send a knight to serve at his court for a year and a day. If I cannot do so,

I am dishonored; yet I am old and have no sons."

"I am strong and healthy," said Stanuta. "Change me into a young man by your magic arts, and I shall go to the Sultan."

"Alas," answered her father, "my skill does not go so far."

"Then I will tell you what you must do," said Stanuta. "Give me a horse and arms; let my hair be cut like a man's, and I shall go."

At first the old knight protested, but presently he agreed to his daughter's plan. Stanuta had her long hair cut off, and her father gave her one of the finest horses in his stable, and the best of weapons and armor. But on the morning she was to start for the Sultan's palace, the old knight rode out ahead of her secretly until he came to a bridge at the boundary of his lands. There he changed himself into the likeness of a blue boar, and hid in the woods beside the river.

When Stanuta reached the bridge, the seeming boar charged out, snorting and pawing the ground. She screamed with terror, turned her horse's head around, and galloped back to the castle.

Next the knight's second daughter, whose name was Roxanda, asked for arms and a horse, so that she might go to the Sultan and serve him in her father's place. She swore that she would ride straight to the palace, and that no boar would turn her from her path. So her father gave her a good horse, and well-made weapons and armor, and Roxanda had her hair cut short like a man's. On the day she was to set out, the old knight went ahead of her as before to the river, changed himself into the likeness of a red lion, and hid among the trees.

When Roxanda came to the bridge, the seeming lion leapt out at her, roaring and lashing its tail. She was struck so dumb with fright that she could not utter a word. Shaking like a poplar tree in the wind, she turned her horse and galloped home to the castle.

Now the knight's youngest daughter, who was called Mizilca, asked that she might have a horse and arms, and she would have her hair cut off and go to the Sultan. But her father refused, saying, "My dear daughter, how can you hope to succeed where your sisters, who are older and stronger than you, have failed? Stay home, and keep your long hair." Mizilca would not listen to him, but kept begging to go, saying that no boar or lion would stand in her way. At last, to be rid of her pleading, her father gave her a rusty sword and lance, and allowed her to saddle an old grey horse that had done nothing for years but pull the cart. On the morning she was to set out, he left the castle before her, took on the likeness of a green dragon, and concealed himself in the trees by the river.

When Mizilca came to the bridge, the dragon

rushed out at her, breathing smoke and fire. Mizilca did not falter, but put spurs to her horse and galloped at him; and the seeming dragon had to run away into the woods to escape being pierced by a real lance. Mizilca did not pursue him, but crossed the bridge and rode on.

Arriving at the palace, Mizilca went before the Sultan, bowed low, and told him that she was the old knight's son, come to serve him for a year and a day. The Sultan looked her up and down, and thought to himself that this was no youth at all, but a maiden. Yet Mizilca stood so straight and spoke out so boldly that he doubted his own eyes. So he welcomed her and admitted her into his company of knights.

The weeks passed, and the Sultan saw that Mizilca could ride and fight and shoot with bow and arrow as well as any of his knights. Yet still, whenever he looked at her, he suspected that she was no man. At last he went to a wise-woman and asked how he could discover whether Mizilca was a youth or a maiden. The wise-woman advised him to have merchants come to the palace while Mizilca was out hunting, and place on one side of the great hall rich cloths and embroideries of silk and velvet, and on the other side all kinds of swords and daggers. "If the knight is a maiden," said the wise-woman, "she will be drawn to the cloths, and pay no heed to the weapons."

And so it was done. But when Mizilca came into the hall and saw the goods laid out, she suspected that the Sultan was testing her. She ignored the silks and velvets and went straight to the weapons, feeling the edges of the blades and making passes with the swords in the air as if fighting.

Time went on, and though Mizilca continued to excel at all knightly pursuits, the Sultan was still not satisfied that she was a man. He went again to the wise-woman, and she advised him to have his cook prepare kasha for dinner, and mix a spoonful of pearls into Mizilca's portion. "If the knight is a maiden," said she, "she will pick out the pearls and save them."

And so it was done. But again Mizilca was too clever for the Sultan. She took the pearls out of the kasha and cast them under the table as if they had been pebbles.

At last the year and a day had passed, and it was time for Mizilca to return home. The Sultan came out to bid her farewell, and said to her, "Mizilca, you have served me well, and paid the debt your father owed. Before you go, answer me one question. Are you a youth or a maiden?" Mizilca did not answer him, but mounted her horse and rode out through the palace gate. Then she turned and opened wide her shirt so that all could see she was a woman, calling out:

High and mighty Sultan, praised be!
Though your word is law o'er land and sea,
I know more of you than you of me.

Then she spurred her horse, and rode off toward her father's castle, where she was welcomed with much joy and feasting.

The tale of the girl who disguises herself as a man and goes off to war in place of her father appears in songs from many parts of Europe. This version is based on a Roumanian ballad. Kasha is a large-grained cereal made from buckwheat.

THE BAKER'S DAUGHTER

There was once a baker who had two daughters. Though they were twins, yet they were as different as summer and winter. One was generous and good-natured while the other was selfish, greedy, and cross.

On a cold evening when the wind swept the streets like a broom, the good-natured daughter was serving in the baker's shop. A poor, ragged old woman came in, leaning on a staff, and asked if she might have a bit of dough. "Certainly, granny," said the girl, and she pulled off a large piece. And might she bake it in the oven? asked the old woman. "Yes, surely," said the baker's daughter.

The old woman sat in the corner and seemed to sleep until the bread was done. "Wake up, granny," said the girl; and then she cried out, "Why, look! The loaf has doubled in size."

"And so shall it always be for you, because of your generous heart," said the old woman, who was really a fairy in disguise. She threw off her cloak and stood up, all tall and shining, and touched the girl with her staff. And from that day on, every loaf of bread or cake or pie the baker's daughter put into the oven came out twice as large.

Time went on, and one evening the ill-natured daughter was serving in the baker's shop. The same ragged old woman shuffled in, leaning on her staff, and asked for a piece of dough. The girl grudgingly gave her a small bit, for her father had told her she must be kind to beggars. And might she bake it in the oven? asked the old woman. "Oh, very well, if you must," answered the baker's daughter.

So the old woman sat in the corner and seemed to sleep. When the bread was done, the baker's daughter opened the oven door, and saw that the dough had doubled in size. "That's too large for the likes of her," she said, and set the loaf aside for herself. She pulled off another piece of dough half the size of the first, and put it into the oven.

Presently the bread was done, and the baker's

daughter opened the oven door and saw that the dough had swelled so that this loaf was twice the size of the first one. "That's far too large for the likes of her," she said, and set it aside with the other. Then she pulled off a tiny bit of dough, hardly as big as her thumb, and shoved it into the oven.

But when she opened the door again, the old woman's tiny bit of dough had swelled up so much it almost filled the oven, and it was all shiny with sugar and full of currants and raisins. "That's far too large and far too fine for the likes of her," said the baker's daughter, and she put the third loaf aside with the other two.

Now the old woman opened her eyes and sat up, and asked if her bread was done.

"It was burnt up in the oven, hoo-hoo," said the girl, laughing.

"Is that all you have to say to me?" asked the old woman.

"Hoo-hoo, what else should I say?" cried the baker's daughter, laughing still.

"And so shall it always be for you," cried the fairy, and she threw off her cloak and stood up tall and shining. "Henceforth you shall say nothing else but *whoo-whoo*." She struck the baker's daughter with her staff, and the girl turned into an owl, and flew out hooting into the night.

This old English tale is the source of Ophelia's lines in **Hamlet***: "They say the owl was a baker's daughter. Lord, we know what we are, but know not what we may be." In some versions, the fairy is replaced by a saint or Our Lord.*

THE
MASTERMAID

O NCE upon a time there was a king's son who went out into the world to seek his fortune. After he had traveled for many days he came one night to a giant's castle. He knocked at the door and asked for work, and the giant took him into his service.

In the morning the giant told the prince to clean out the stable. "After you have finished that," said he, "you may do as you like and go where you will the rest of the day. Only stay out of the room in the tower, if you value your life. I am an easy master if you do as you are told; but if you disobey me, I will kill you." And the giant laughed loudly and went off to herd his goats.

"Sure enough, it is an easy master I have got," thought the prince, and he walked about the yard, humming and singing to himself and enjoying the morning air, for he thought there was plenty of time to do his work. At length, however, he decided he might as well get the thing over with. So he took up a pitchfork and went to the stable. But for every forkful of dirt and straw he flung out of the door, ten forkfuls came flying in at him, so that soon he had hardly room to stand. He labored as fast as he could till he was worn out, but the stables were dirtier than before.

At last the prince threw down his pitchfork in despair and went back to the castle, all covered with dirt and straw. He resolved to run away before the giant came back to kill him, but first he thought he would go to the room in the tower and see what was there. So he climbed the stairs and pushed open the door. And there, sitting by the window, was a girl so lovely that he had never seen her like.

"In God's name, who are you?" cried she.

"I am the new servingman," said the prince.

"Then Heaven help you!" said the girl.

"Would that it could," replied the young man. "For though I have tried all morning to clean out the stable, it is a hundred times dirtier than before I began."

"Very likely," said the girl. "But you may manage it yet. I will tell you what you must do: You must turn the pitchfork around and work with the handle, and the dirt will fly out of itself."

The prince went back to the stable and did as she had advised; and he had hardly begun when the whole place was as clean as if it had been scoured. Then, since it was still early, he returned to the tower. He and the girl spent the rest of the day in talking together, so that the time seemed short until she said that he must leave her.

So evening drew on, and home came the giant with his goats.

"Have you cleaned the stable?" said he, grinning.

"Yes, master, it's all clean and fresh."

"We'll see about that," growled the giant, and he strode off to the stable, where he found things just as the prince had said.

"And how did you manage that?" said he.

"I could not get the dirt out with the pitchfork, so I turned it around and worked with the handle," said the prince.

"You must have been talking to my Mastermaid," said the giant, "for you never got that out of your own head."

"Mastermaid?" asked the prince, looking stupid as an owl. "What is that?"

"Never you mind," said the giant. "You'll know soon enough."

The next morning, before the giant went off with his

goats, he told the prince to go and bring home his horse, which was grazing on the hillside, and after that he might have the rest of the day to himself. "I am an easy master," said he, grinning, "if you do as you are told. But if you fail, I will wring your neck."

The prince was eager to see the Mastermaid again, but he decided that first he would do his work. So he went up the hillside. When he saw the horse, he thought it would be an easy task to bring it home, for he had ridden far wilder-looking ones before. But when he got near it, the horse began to stamp and rear, and fire and smoke came out of its nostrils as if it were a flaming torch, so that the prince's clothes and hair were singed.

He went back to the castle, climbed up to the tower, and told the Mastermaid what had happened.

"Very likely," said she. "I will tell you what you must do. Take the old bridle which hangs by the stable door, and throw it into the horse's mouth, and then you will be able to ride him."

The prince did as she had told him; when the horse came at him snorting and flaming, he threw the bit into its mouth, and the fires went out and the animal stood there as quiet as a lamb. He rode it home and put it in the stable, and then he went back to the Mastermaid and spent the rest of the day with her. And the more they were together, the better they liked each other; indeed the prince would have forgotten about the giant if the Mastermaid hadn't reminded him that evening was coming on.

Presently the giant came home with his goats, and the first words he said were, "Have you brought my horse down from the hill?"

"Yes, that I have," said the prince.

"We'll see about that," said the giant, and he hurried off to the stable, where he found the horse munching his oats.

"And how did you manage that?" growled the giant.

"It was nothing," said the prince. "He did not want to come at first, but I threw the bit into his mouth, and he quieted down nicely."

"You have been talking to my Mastermaid, I swear it," said the giant. "You never thought of that yourself."

"Mastermaid?" said the prince, looking foolish. "You said that yesterday, and today it's the same story. I should like to see that thing, master."

"You'll see it soon enough," said the giant.

The third day, before the giant went off with his goats, he said to the prince, "Today you must go down to Hell and fetch my firetax. When you have got it you can have the rest of the day to yourself, for I am an easy master. But if it isn't here when I come home, I will wring your neck and eat you for supper." And he laughed loudly.

This time the prince did not even try to do his work, for he did not know the way to Hell; instead he went straight to the Mastermaid.

"You must take a sack," said she, "and go to the cliff over yonder under the hill, and knock on the face of the rock with the club that lies there. Then one will come out, all shining with fire. Tell him your errand; and when he asks how much you want, you must say, 'As much as I can carry.' "

So the prince went to the hillside and knocked with the club as hard as he could. The rock split open, and out came one shining with flames and with sparks of fire coming from his eyes and nose.

"What is your will?" cried he.

"I have come for the giant's firetax," said the prince.

"How much will you have?" asked the fiery one.

"Only as much as I can carry," said the prince.

"It's well for you that you asked for no more," said the other. "Come with me, and you shall have it."

So the prince followed the fiery one down into the rock, until they came to a chamber where heaps of gold and silver lay about like stones in a gravel pit. The prince filled his sack as full as he could carry, and took it home.

Then he went back to the Mastermaid. By the end of the day he was so much in love with her, and she with him, that he would have sat there till now if the Mastermaid had not reminded him that the giant would soon be coming.

When the giant came into the yard with his goats, he cried out, "Have you been to Hell after my firetax?"

"Oh, yes, that I have," said the prince. "There it is."

"We'll see about that," said the giant, and he opened the sack, which was so full that gold and silver spilled from it.

"And how did you get this?" he roared.

"I went to the rock over yonder, and knocked on it."

"You have been talking to my Mastermaid!" roared the giant.

"Mastermaid?" said the prince stupidly. "What is a Mastermaid? You keep talking of this creature, but you never show it to me."

"Well, you shall see it now," cried the giant. He seized the prince and trussed him up with a rope as if he were a chicken, and then he called the Mastermaid down from the tower, and said to her, "I am tired of this fool. Cut him up and boil him in the big pot; and when the stew is ready, wake me." And he laid himself down on the bench and began to snore, so that it sounded like thunder in the hills.

The Mastermaid freed the prince, and then she cut her little finger with a knife and let three drops of blood fall on a three-legged stool. Then she gathered all the old rags and bones and rubbish she could lay hands on, and put them into the pot. She took the bag of gold and silver, and she and the prince ran away from the giant's castle as fast as they could go.

After the giant had slept a good while, he began to stretch himself as he lay on the bench, and called out, "Will dinner soon be done?"

"Only just begun," answered the first drop of blood on the stool, in the voice of the Mastermaid.

So the giant lay down to sleep again. He slumbered a long time, but at last he began to toss about a little, and cried out, "Is it ready now?"

"Half done, I vow," said the second drop of blood.

The giant turned over on his other side and fell asleep again, and when he had slept many, many hours, he began to stir and stretch, and called out, "How is my meat?"

"Ready to eat," said the third drop of blood.

Then the giant rose up, rubbing his eyes. He could not see who might be talking to him, so he called for the Mastermaid, but there was no answer. He took up a spoon and went to the pot to try the stew, but as soon as he had tasted it he spat it out, for it was nothing but old rags and bones boiled up together. When he saw this, the giant knew how things had gone. He raged and roared through all the rooms of the castle, looking for the prince and the Mastermaid, but they were far away by now. The giant was so angry that he howled and raged and stamped on the floor until he burst into little pieces.

As for the prince and the Mastermaid, they reached his father's kingdom in safety and lived happily ever after.

<hr />

This is an abridged version of a very long Norwegian story, almost a saga, in which the Mastermaid overcomes a series of obstacles and enemies by a combination of wit and magical powers.

MOLLY WHUPPIE

O NCE upon a time there was a man and wife who had so many children that they could not feed them all. So they took their three youngest daughters into the forest and left them there. The girls walked and walked for hours; it began to be dark, and they were hungry. At last they saw the lights of a house and made their way toward it. They knocked at the door, and a woman opened it and asked them what they wanted.

"Oh, please," said they. "Could we come in and have a bit to eat?"

No, said the woman, they could not do that; for her husband was a giant, and he would kill them if he found them there.

"Please, ma'am," said the girls. "We'll just stay a little while, and be gone before he comes home."

So she let them in, and sat them down before the

fire, and gave them some bread and milk. But just as they
had begun to eat, there was a great knock at the door,
and a dreadful voice cried:

"Fee, fie, fo, fum,
I smell the blood of some earthly one.

Who have you there, wife?"

"Oh," said his wife, "it's just three poor lassies who
were cold and hungry, and they'll be going soon. Let
them be."

The giant said nothing, but gobbled up a huge supper; then he ordered them to spend the night.

Now this ogre had three daughters of his own, and
they were going to share their bed with the three strang-
ers, the youngest of whom was called Molly Whuppie.
Molly was a very clever girl, and she noticed that before
they all went to bed the giant put straw ropes around her
and her sisters' necks and gold chains around the necks
of his own daughters. So Molly stayed awake, and when
the rest were sleeping sound, she slipped out of bed, and
took the straw ropes off her own and her sisters' necks,
and the gold chains off those of the giant's daughters.
Then she put the straw ropes on the giant's daughters
and the gold chains on herself and her sisters, and lay
down again.

In the middle of the night, up rose the giant armed with a great club. He came over to the bed and felt for the necks circled with straw, for it was too dark to see. When he found them, he took his own three daughters out of bed and beat them with the club until they were dead. Then he lay down again, thinking he had managed fine.

Molly thought it was time she and her sisters were out of that, so she woke them and told them to be quiet, and they slipped out of the house. They ran and they ran and never stopped until morning, when they saw a grand house before them. It was the king's palace. So Molly went in, and told her story to the king.

"Well, Molly," said he, "you are a clever girl, and you have managed well. But if you would go back to the giant's house and bring me the magic sword that hangs on his bedpost, I would marry your oldest sister to my oldest son."

"I will try," said Molly.

So she went back, and slipped into the giant's house, and crept under his bed. Presently the giant came home, gobbled up a big supper, and went to bed. Molly waited until he was snoring, and then she crept out and reached up over the sleeping giant and got down the sword; but just then he woke. She ran out of the door, and the giant after her. And she ran, and he ran, till they reached the

Bridge of One Hair. And she ran over it, but he could not, and he said:

> "Woe to ye, Molly Whuppie!
> Never ye come again."

And she said:

> "Twice more, churl,
> I'll come to Spain."

Then Molly took the giant's sword to the king, and her oldest sister was married to his oldest son.

"Well, Molly," said the king. "You are a clever girl. But if you would go back to the giant's house and bring me the magic purse of gold that he keeps under his pillow, I would marry your second sister to my second son."

"I will try," said Molly.

So she went back, and slipped into the giant's house, and crept under his bed, and waited till he had eaten his supper and was fast asleep. As soon as she heard him snoring, she crept out, slipped her hand under the pillow, and drew out the purse; but just then he woke. Molly ran out of the door, and the giant after her. And she ran, and he ran, till they reached the Bridge of One

Hair. And she ran over it, but he could not, and he said:

> "Woe to ye, Molly Whuppie!
> Never ye come again."

And she said:

> "Once more, churl,
> I'll come to Spain."

Then Molly took the purse to the king, and her second sister was married to his second son.

"Well, Molly," said the king. "You are a very clever girl. But if you would go back once more to the giant's house and bring me the ring of invisibility he wears on his finger, I would marry you to my youngest son."

"I will try," said Molly.

So off she went to the giant's house, and hid herself under his bed. As soon as she heard him snoring loud, she crept out, and reached across the bed, and took hold of his hand. She pulled and she pulled until she got off the ring; but just then the giant woke, and caught her fast by the hand.

"Now I've got you, Molly Whuppie!" said the giant. "And as you're so clever, answer me this: If I had served you as you've served me, what would you do with me?"

Molly considered how she might escape, and then

she said, "Why, I would put you into a sack, and I would put the cat and the dog in with you. Then I would hang the sack on the wall and go into the woods, and bring home the biggest and thickest stick I could find, and beat the sack till you were dead."

"Well, Molly," said the giant, "I'll do just that to you."

So he got a sack and put Molly into it, and the cat and the dog with her, and he hung the sack up on the wall, and went off to the wood to choose a stick.

As soon as he had gone, Molly began to sing, "Oh, if you could only see what I see!"

"Oh," said the giant's wife. "What do you see, Molly?"

But Molly never answered a word but "Oh, if you could see what I see!" The giant's wife pleaded with Molly to take her into the sack so that she could see what Molly saw. So at last Molly agreed, and the giant's wife cut a hole in the sack with a pair of scissors, and Molly jumped down. Then she helped the giant's wife up into the sack, and sewed up the hole.

The giant's wife saw nothing in the sack, and began to ask to get down again; but Molly never answered her, only hid herself behind the door. Presently home came the giant, with a great big tree in his hand, and he took down the sack and began to beat it.

"It's me, man!" cried the giant's wife, but what with the dog's barking and the cat's meowing, he did not know her voice. Molly did not want the giant's wife to be killed, so she came out from behind the door. The giant saw her, and ran after her. And she ran, and he ran, till they reached the Bridge of One Hair. And she ran over it, but he could not, and he said:

> "Woe to ye, Molly Whuppie!
> Never ye come again."

And she said:

> "Never more, churl,
> I'll come to Spain."

Then Molly took the ring to the king and was married to his youngest son; and she never saw the giant again.

<hr />

This female version of "Jack and the Beanstalk" comes from Aberdeen, Scotland—not Spain. The rhyme with which Molly taunts the giant is probably the tag from an old children's game, the Scottish equivalent of

> *"Rover, red rover,*
> *Once more I'll come over."*

THE HAND
OF GLORY

LATE one evening a solitary traveler in woman's dress arrived at an inn on a lonely road in the north of England, and asked for supper. She said that she did not want a room, for she must be on her way again in a few hours. The people of the house went to bed, but they arranged for a servant girl to sit up until the traveler had gone and to lock the door after her.

When all the house was quiet, the stranger said, "Lie down and get some sleep, child, and I will wake you before I leave." So the girl, whose name was Katie, went and lay on a bench by the fire. But before she closed her eyes, she happened to look across the room at the traveler, and beneath the gown she saw a man's shoes and trousers. Katie was alarmed, and could not think what this meant, so she determined to stay awake and watch the stranger. She put her arm over her face, pretended to doze off, and even began to snore.

As soon as the traveler was satisfied that Katie was sleeping soundly, he stood up and pulled off his woman's clothes and wig. Next he took out of his bag a dead man's hand, all dry and withered. He set it upright on the table, struck a match, and put the flame to the four fingers and thumb one after another, and they flared up and began to burn like candles. Then he said aloud:

"Hand of Glory, Hand of Glory!
Let those who are asleep, be asleep.
Let those who are awake, be awake."

Then Katie, watching from under her arm, saw him go to the door, open it, and whistle. Soon another evil-looking man came in, and together the two robbers began putting all the silver spoons and plates of the inn into their bags. When they had taken everything of value, they went into the next room.

Katie was terrified now, but she thought that she must do something, so she crept up the back stairs and tried to wake her master and the other men of the house. But she could not rouse them—all slept as if they were dead, for the spell of the dead man's hand was on them.

Though she feared for her life, Katie tiptoed down the back stairs again. There was the Hand of Glory still burning in the empty kitchen, and she could hear the robbers at work in the next room. They were not troubling to be quiet or to speak low, for they thought that every soul in the house was sound asleep.

Katie went up to the table and blew upon the burning hand as hard as she could; but it would not go out. She took up a pitcher of water and cast it over the flames; but still they burned. Then she poured the beer that remained from the robber's supper upon the hand, and that was worst of all, for it blazed up higher than before. At last in despair she caught up a jug of milk; and when she threw this on the flames they went out at once.

Katie did not wait to see what would happen next, but ran upstairs again; and this time she had no trouble rousing the whole household. The robbers were surprised and captured, and the inn was saved.

The belief in the powers of a hanged man's hand, or "Hand of Glory," goes back at least to seventeenth-century England. Once lit, the Hand of Glory can usually only be extinguished by saying the proper spell—or with milk, which has power over evil spells.

MAID MALEEN

O NCE long ago there was a great king's daughter whose name was Maid Maleen. A young prince came courting her; she returned his love, and they were agreed to wed. But her father would not have it, for he wished to marry Maid Maleen to a neighboring king. He told his daughter to send the young man away, but Maid Maleen refused. She swore to her father that she would never marry the man he had chosen, or any other on this earth except the young prince.

The king became very angry, and ordered his workmen to put up a tower with no windows, into which not a single ray of sunlight or moonlight could ever shine. When the tower was finished he said to his daughter, "You shall be shut up here for seven years. Then I'll come and see if you are still so obstinate." Food and drink enough for seven years were brought to the tower;

then Maid Maleen and her lady-in-waiting were led in and the door was walled up behind them. There they sat in the darkness, not knowing when the sun rose or set. The prince who loved Maid Maleen walked round and round the dark tower for a long time, calling out her name; but she did not reply, for no sound came through the thick walls. At last he went sadly away, believing that she was dead.

Slowly, slowly, the time passed, and Maid Maleen could tell by the dwindling of the store of food and drink that the seven years were drawing to an end. Now she and her lady-in-waiting expected to hear the sound of hammers knocking down the walls to set them free, but they heard nothing. The king seemed to have forgotten them. When there was only enough food left for a few days, Maid Maleen said, "If we stay here, we will die of hunger. Let us see if we can make a hole in the wall." She took the bread knife and began to dig and scrape at the mortar between the stones, and when she grew tired, the lady-in-waiting took her turn.

After long labor, they managed to loosen one stone, and then a second and a third. When three days had passed a ray of light shone into their darkness, and at last the opening was large enough for them to look through. It was a fair spring day—a cool breeze was blowing, the sky was blue—but beneath it all was desolation. The

castle lay in ruins, and the countryside round about was burnt and laid waste as far as the eye could see.

Maid Maleen and her lady-in-waiting continued to work on the hole, and as soon as it was large enough, they squeezed through and jumped down. But where were they to go? The king's enemies had attacked the town, driven out or killed all the people, and set fire to whatever remained. Maid Maleen and her companion walked on and on without finding a single cottage standing or meeting a living soul; they slept under hedges and ate the weeds that grew by the roadside.

After they had wandered on a long while, they came to a kingdom by the sea. They went from house to house begging for work, but they were always turned away, until at last they came to the royal palace. And there they were given work in the kitchen as scullery maids.

Now it happened that the son of the king of this land was the young prince who had loved Maid Maleen. For seven years he had mourned for her, and refused to marry. But at last he gave in to the wishes of his parents, and said that he would wed whomever they chose. And they had found for him a princess who had great riches, but whose face was as ugly as her heart was cold.

The wedding had been set, and the bride had arrived, but she had not shown herself, for she feared that if the prince were to see her he would change his mind.

So she shut herself in her room, and Maid Maleen had to bring up her meals from the kitchen.

When the wedding day came, the ugly princess said to Maid Maleen, "You are a lucky girl, and I'm going to do you a great honor. I've sprained my ankle and can't walk to church. If you will swear not to speak a word to anyone, you may put on the bridal dress and take my place today." But Maid Maleen refused, saying, "I want no honor that is not mine by right." Then the princess grew angry and said, "If you don't do as I tell you, you slut, I will have your head cut off."

So Maid Maleen had to put on the bride's dress, and swear that she would say nothing to any man or woman that day.

When she entered the great hall, everyone marveled at her grace and beauty. The prince, too, was amazed. "She is like my Maid Maleen, who lies dead in the dark tower," he thought. He greeted her courteously, but Maid Maleen did not reply. The prince thought she was shy, so he took her by the hand and led her toward the church.

As they came out of the castle, they passed a nettle bush, and Maid Maleen said:

"Nettles, stand aside;
I am the true bride."

"What did you say?" asked the prince.

"Nothing," answered Maid Maleen. "I was only speaking to the nettle bush."

They walked along by the edge of the sea, and she said:

> "Sea, hold back your tide;
> I am the true bride."

"What did you say?" asked the prince.

"Nothing," she replied. "I was only speaking to the waves."

At length they came to the church, and Maid Maleen said:

> "Church doors, open wide;
> I am the true bride."

"What did you say?" whispered the prince.

"Nothing," she answered. "I was only speaking to the church doors."

So they went in, and the priest joined their hands and married them. The prince kissed Maid Maleen, and put a gold ring on her finger, and led her back to the palace. All through the wedding supper and the dancing she smiled at him, but she did not utter one word to anyone.

Then Maid Maleen went to the princess's room, took off the bride's dress, and put on her ragged clothes again; but she had to keep the gold ring, for it fitted so tightly to her finger that she could not get it off.

When it was time for the prince to come to the ugly princess, she dimmed the lamps and veiled her face so that she could hardly be seen. After the courtiers had left them alone, the prince said to her, "What was it that you said to the nettle bush today?"

"What do you mean?" said the princess. "I don't talk to nettle bushes."

"Well, then," said the prince. "What did you say to the sea?"

"Nothing, of course," answered the princess crossly. "I don't talk to the sea."

"Well, then," said the prince. "What did you say to the church doors?"

"Nothing, you fool," answered the ugly princess. "I don't talk to doors."

"Then you are not the true bride," said the prince.

"Oh, yes, I am," said the princess.

"Then where is the ring I gave you in church today?" cried the prince, seizing her hand.

"I lost it," said the princess.

But the prince pulled her veil off, and when he saw her face he cried out in horror, "Who are you? How did you get here?"

"I am your betrothed bride," said the ugly princess, "but I was ill today, so I ordered the scullery maid to put on my dress and go to church with you in my place."

"Where is she?" asked the prince. "I must see her."

"Very well," said the princess. She went out and called to the guards, "The scullery maid is a thief; she has stolen my ring! Take her down to the courtyard and cut off her head."

The guards seized Maid Maleen, and started to drag her away, but she screamed so loud that the prince heard her and came running from his room. He shouted at the guards and ordered them to release her. "Tell me who you are," he said. "I once loved a girl called Maid Maleen who is long dead, and you are so like her that you might be twins."

"I am Maid Maleen," she answered. "I was shut in the dark tower for seven years, but I did not die. My father's kingdom was destroyed, but I escaped and came here. Today I was married to you in church, and now I am your lawful wife."

The prince embraced Maid Maleen with great joy, and ordered that the ugly princess should be sent home to her own land. And he and his true bride lived happily together in the kingdom by the sea for the rest of their lives.

The tower where Maid Maleen had been imprisoned remained standing for many years. When the children passed it, they sang:

> "Sunflower, moonflower,
> Who sits within the tower?
> Within there sits a princess fair,
> Nobody can see her there.
> No hammer can break down the wall,
> No storm can make the tower fall.
> Oak-tree, willow-tree,
> Come and follow after me."

This is an adaptation of one of the tales of the Brothers Grimm which is seldom included in modern selections from their works. In a Norwegian version of the same story, the princess is buried under a mound of earth, and it takes her twelve years to dig her way out.

KATE
CRACKERNUTS

O NCE upon a time there was a king and a queen, such as there have been in many lands. The king had a daughter, and the queen had one also. And though they were no kin, yet the two girls loved each other better than sisters. But the queen was jealous because the king's daughter Ann was prettier than her own daughter Kate. She wished to find some way to spoil Ann's beauty; so she went to consult the henwife, who was a witch.

"Aye, I can help you," said the henwife. "Send her to me in the morning; but make sure she does not eat anything before she comes." And she put her big black pot on the fire, and boiled a sheep's hide and bones in it, with other nasty things.

Early in the morning the queen told Ann to go to the henwife and fetch some eggs. But as she left the house, Ann took up a crust of bread to eat on the way. When she asked for the eggs, the witch said to her, "Lift the lid off that pot, and you will find what you need." So the king's daughter lifted the lid; but nothing came out of the pot except an evil smell. "Go back to your mother, and tell her to keep her pantry door better locked," said the henwife.

When the queen heard this message, she knew that Ann must have had something to eat. So she locked her pantry, and next morning sent the girl off again. But as Ann went through the garden she saw the gardener picking vegetables. Being a friendly girl, she stopped to speak with him, and he gave her a handful of peas to eat. And when she got to the henwife's house, everything happened just as before.

On the third morning the queen went down to the gate with Ann, so as to be certain she would eat nothing on her way to the witch. And this time, when Ann lifted the lid of the pot, off jumped her own pretty head, and on jumped a sheep's head in its place.

When the queen looked out her window and saw Ann coming back with her sheep's head, she laughed out loud with satisfaction. "Look at your sister," she said to her own daughter Kate. "Now you are the prettiest by far."

"That pleases me not," said Kate. And she would say no more to her mother, but wrapped a fine linen cloth around her sister's head, and took her by the hand, and they went out into the world together to seek their fortunes.

They walked on far, and further than I can tell, eating the berries that grew by the roadside, and the nuts that Kate gathered in her apron and cracked as they went along. At last they came to a tall castle. Kate knocked at the castle door, and begged a night's lodging for herself and her sister.

Now the king and queen of that place had two sons, and the elder of them was ill with a strange wasting illness. Though he ate heartily, and slept late, yet every morning he was more thin and pale than the evening before. The king had offered a peck of gold to anyone who would sit up with his son for three nights and find out what ailed him. Many had tried, but all had failed. But Kate was a clever girl and a brave girl, and she offered to sit up with the prince. She did not go boldly into his room as the others had, but arranged to have herself hidden there in the evening, and watched to see what would happen.

Till midnight all was quiet. As twelve o'clock struck, however, the sick prince rose, dressed himself, and went downstairs. He walked as if in a dream, and did not seem to notice Kate following after him. He went to the stables, saddled his horse, called his hound, and mounted.

Kate leapt up behind him, but he paid her no heed. Away
went the horse with the prince and Kate through the
greenwood, where the nuts were ripe. As they passed
under the trees, Kate picked the nuts and filled her
apron with them, for she did not know when they might
come back again.

They rode on and on, till they came to a green hill.
There the prince drew rein and spoke for the first time,
saying, "Open, open, green hill, and let in the young
prince with his horse and his hound."

And Kate added, "and his lady behind him."

Then the hill opened, and they passed into a great
hall filled with bright light that seemed to come from
nowhere, and a strange music playing. Kate slipped
down off the horse, and hid herself behind the door. At
once the prince was surrounded by fairy ladies who led
him off to the dance. All night he danced without stop-
ping, first with one and then with another, and though
he looked weary and worn they would not let him leave
off.

At last the cock crew, and the prince made haste to
mount his horse. Kate jumped up behind, and they rode
home, where the prince lay down to sleep paler and
more ill than before.

The next night when the clock struck twelve the
same thing happened; and again Kate rode through the

forest behind the prince into the green hill. This time she did not watch the dancing, but crept near to where some of the fairy people were sitting together and a fairy baby was playing with a wand.

"What news in the world above?" said one.

"No news," said the other, "but that a sad lady with a sheep's head has come to lodge in the castle."

"Is that so?" said the first, laughing. "If only she knew that three strokes of that wand would make her as fair as she ever was."

Kate heard this, and thought that she must have the wand. She took some nuts and rolled them toward the baby from behind the door, till the baby ran after the nuts and let the wand fall, and Kate snatched it up and put it in her apron. At cockcrow she rode home as before, and the prince lay down to sleep, looking weary and ill unto death. Kate ran to her room and tapped her sister Ann three times with the wand; and the sheep's head jumped off and Ann had her own pretty head again. Then Ann dressed herself and went into the great hall of the castle where all welcomed her, and the king's younger son thought that he had never seen anyone sweeter and prettier in his life.

On the third night, Kate watched the sick prince again, and rode behind him to the green hill. Again she hid behind the door and listened to the talk of the fairy people. This time the little child was playing with a yellow bird.

"What news in the world above?" said one fairy to the other.

"No news, but that the king and queen are at their wits' end to know what ails their eldest son."

"Is that so?" said the first fairy, laughing. "If only they knew that three bites of that birdie would free him from the spell and make him as well as ever he was."

Kate heard this, and thought that she must have the yellow birdie. So she rolled nuts to the baby until he ran after them and dropped the birdie, and she caught it up and put it in her apron.

At cockcrow they set off for home again, and as soon as they got there Kate plucked and cooked the yellow birdie and took it to the prince. He was lying in bed more dead than alive after his night's dancing; but when he smelled the dish, he opened his eyes and said, "Oh, I wish I had a bite of that birdie!" So Kate gave him a bite, and he rose up on his elbow.

By and by he cried out again, "Oh, if only I had another bite of that birdie!" Kate gave him another bite, and the prince sat up on his bed and looked about him. Then he said again, "Oh, if only I had a third bite of that birdie!" Kate gave him a third bite, and he got out of bed, well and strong again. He dressed himself and sat down by the fire, and Kate told him all that had passed. They stayed there till it was full morning, and the people of the castle came in and found them cracking nuts together.

So Kate married the king's eldest son, and Ann married his brother, and they lived happily together ever after.

This Scottish tale is one of many that have been cited as proof that the fairies were the original prehistoric inhabitants of the British Isles, little folk who built their houses underground. Some of the grass-covered mounds that are thought to have been their dwellings can still be seen in the Orkney Islands, where "Kate Crackernuts" was recorded.

THE
SLEEPING PRINCE

ONCE upon a time there
lived a king and queen
who had one daughter whom they loved dearly. Now on
a day in winter, when the countryside was covered with
snow, she was sitting at her window sewing. As she
sewed she pricked her finger, and a drop of red blood fell
on the sill in the golden sunlight. And a bird in a tree
outside sang:

> "Gold and white and red,
> The Prince sleeps in his bed."

The princess was struck by these words, and called
out, "Pray, little bird, sing again!" And the bird sang:

> "White and red and gold,
> He shall sleep till time is old."

The princess cried, "Ah, little bird, sing again!" And the bird sang:

"Red and gold and white,
He wakes on St. John's Night."

"But what does your song mean?" asked the princess. So the bird told her that in a castle far, far away, and further still, there dwelt the noblest and handsomest prince in the world, with skin as white as snow and lips as red as blood and hair as golden as the sun. A spell had been cast over him, so that he fell into a deep sleep from which he could wake only once a year, on St. John's Night. And thus it would be until the end of time. But if a maiden were to watch beside his bed, so that he might see her when he woke, then the spell would be broken.

"And where is this castle?" asked the Princess.

"I do not know," said the bird, "except that it is far, far away, and further still, so that to get there you must wear out a pair of iron shoes."

Days passed, and the princess could not forget the song the bird had sung. At last she said to herself that she must and would go to find the Sleeping Prince, and free him from the spell. But as she knew that her father and mother would never consent to let her make such a journey, she said nothing to them. She had a pair of iron shoes made, and as soon as they were ready, late one night, she put them on and left the palace.

When the king and queen missed her next morning, they sent men to search throughout the country. But the princess eluded her searchers, and got out of the king-dom without being seen by anyone. Her father and mother grieved much, for they thought that she must be dead.

The princess walked on and on in her iron shoes, far, far, and further still, until she came to a great dark forest. She did not turn aside, but went straight on into the forest, and late in the evening she saw a lonely cot-tage. She knocked at the door, and an old woman opened it and asked what she wanted.

"I am searching for the castle of the Sleeping Prince," said the girl. "Do you know where it is?"

"Not I," said the old woman. "But I can give you a bite to eat and a drop to drink, and then you must go back to where you came from, for this is no place for a mortal woman."

"No," said the princess. "I must go on."

"If you must, you must," said the old woman. "Come in, then, my dear, and when my son the West Wind gets home I will ask him if he knows the way. But you must take care he does not see or hear you."

So she let the princess in, and gave her some supper, and hid her in the corner cupboard. Soon there was a rushing and a sighing of rain outside, and in came the West Wind.

"Mother," sighed he, "I smell mortal flesh."

"Oh, my son," said his mother, "don't be angry! It was only a poor girl in iron shoes who came by here today, wanting to know the way to the castle of the Sleeping Prince."

"That I do not know," said the West Wind. "But perhaps my cousin the East Wind may have seen it."

As soon as it was light the next morning the princess started on her journey again. She walked on and on, far, far, and further still, in her iron shoes. The sun scorched her and the rain wetted her. At last late one evening she came to another cottage, where another old woman asked what she wanted.

"I am searching for the castle of the Sleeping Prince," said the princess. "Do you know where it is?"

"Not I," said the old woman. "But I can give you a bite to eat and a drop to drink, and then you must go back to where you came from, for this is no place for a mortal woman."

"No," said the princess. "I must go on."

"If you must, you must," said the old woman. "Come in then, my dear, and when my son the East

Wind gets home I will ask him if he knows the way. But you must take care he does not see or hear you, for he would be very angry." So she let the Princess in, and gave her some supper, and hid her in the corner cupboard.

Soon there was a shrieking and a whirring of dust outside, and in came the East Wind.

"Mother," shrieked he, "I smell mortal flesh!"

"Oh, my son," said his mother, "don't be angry! It was only a poor girl in iron shoes who came by here today, wanting to know the way to the castle of the Sleeping Prince."

"That I do not know," said the East Wind. "But perhaps my cousin the North Wind may have seen it."

As soon as it was light the next morning the Princess started out again. She walked on and on, far, far, and further still, in her iron shoes. The sun scorched her and the rain wetted her, till her fine clothes were worn to rags. At last late one evening she came to another cottage. When the old woman who lived there saw her, she was frightened and tried to send her away.

"No," said the princess. "I must go on, for I am seeking the castle of the Sleeping Prince."

"If you must, you must," said the old woman. "Come in then, my dear, and when my son the North Wind gets home I will ask him if he knows the way. But you must take care he does not see or hear you, for he would kill you."

So she let the princess in, and gave her some supper, and hid her in the corner cupboard. Soon there was a terrible roaring and blowing of snow outside, and in came the North Wind.

"Mother," roared he, "I smell mortal flesh!"

"Oh, my son," said his mother, "don't be angry! It was only a poor ragged girl in iron shoes who came by here today, wanting to know the way to the castle of the Sleeping Prince."

"Well, that is easy," said the North Wind. "The path outside our door leads directly to it."

"Then she will find the castle," said his mother, "for that is the road she took."

"Yes," said the North Wind with a loud laugh, "and little good will it do her, for the gate is guarded by two huge lions who devour all who try to pass through."

"Is there no way for her to enter the castle, then?"

"There is one way," said the North Wind. "If she were to pick two of the white roses that grow by our door and throw them at the lions, they would lie down and let her pass."

As soon as it was light the next morning the princess set out, taking with her two white roses from the bush by the North Wind's door. She walked on and on, far, far,

and further still. The sun scorched her and the rain wetted her and the snow chilled her. At last she looked down, and saw that her iron shoes were worn quite through. She looked up, and saw before her the towers of a castle.

Soon she came to the gate, and saw the two great lions guarding it. When they caught sight of the princess they began to growl and paw the ground and show their teeth, so that she wanted to run away. Yet all the same she went on. Just as the lions began to spring at her she threw the white roses at them; and at once they became tame, and began to purr and rub themselves against her like kittens. The gates opened for the princess, and she walked barefoot into the castle.

Inside she found many rooms, all of them furnished as magnificently as any prince could desire. But what was most strange was that everyone and everything in the castle was asleep, and try as she might the princess could not wake them. The servants were asleep in the hall, the cook and maids in the kitchen, the gardener in the garden, the groom and the horses in the stable, the cows in the barn, the chickens and ducks in the poultry yard, and even the flies on the wall.

The princess searched through all the rooms of the castle, and at last she came to a bedchamber hung with curtains of silver, and on the bed asleep lay the handsomest prince in the world. His skin was white as snow, his lips as red as blood, and his hair golden as the sun.

The princess could not wake him, so she sat down beside his bed. Just as evening fell, a table covered with the most delicious supper appeared before her; and when she had eaten, it vanished. All night long she watched by the sleeping prince. At dawn the table appeared again, and vanished when she had eaten just as before.

The days passed, and the weeks, and the months. Still the princess sat every night by the side of the sleeping prince, waiting for him to wake. At last it came to be St. John's Eve, but she did not know it, for she had lost count of time on her long journey.

At midnight the clock in the tallest tower, which had until then been silent, began to strike. On the stroke of twelve the prince yawned, opened his eyes, and saw the princess sitting beside his bed, barefoot and in rags like a beggar maid.

"At last, the spell has been broken!" he cried.

Now there was a noise and clamor of voices downstairs, a neighing and mooing and clucking and quacking, as everyone in the castle awoke from their long sleep: the servants in the hall, the cook and maids in the kitchen, the gardener in the garden, the groom and the horses in the stable, the cows in the barn, the chickens and ducks in the poultry yard, and even the flies on the wall. But the prince paid no heed to any of this, for he was gazing at the princess.

"Whoever you may be, my life belongs to you," he said. "Will you marry me?"

The princess looked into his eyes, and saw that he was as good and brave as he was beautiful. "With all my heart," she said.

And so they were married with great ceremony and feasting that lasted for three days. Then the prince and princess mounted on the two fastest horses in his stable, and rode to the castle of the king and queen, who were overcome with joy to see their daughter again. As for the prince, though he was surprised to discover that his wife was not a beggar maid after all, he was not happier, for he already loved her more than all the world.

This old Spanish folktale is very much like "Sleeping Beauty" with the sexes reversed. St. John's Night is Midsummer Eve, the shortest night of the year and a time when magic is most powerful.

CAP O'RUSHES

Once there was a very rich gentleman, and he had three daughters. And he thought he would see how fond they were of him. So he said to the eldest, "How much do you love me, my dear?"

"Why," said she, "as much as I love my life."

"That's good," said he.

Then he said to the second, "How much do you love me, my dear?"

"Why," said she, "better than all the world."

"That's good," said he.

Then he said to his youngest daughter, "How much do you love me, my dear?"

"I love you as much as fresh meat loves salt," said she.

"Is that so," said he, very angry. "You don't love me at all, and you'll stay no more in my house." So he drove her out there and then, with nothing but the clothes she was wearing, and shut the door in her face.

The girl wandered away, on and on, weeping and lamenting, till she came to the marshes. There she gathered a heap of rushes, and wove them into a sort of cloak with a hood, which covered her from head to foot and hid her fine dress. Then she went on till she came to a great house, and there she knocked at the kitchen door.

"Do you want a maid?" said she.

"No, we don't," said they.

"But I've got nowhere to go," said she, "and I'll ask no wages, and do any sort of work."

"Well," said the cook, "if you want to wash the pots and scrape the saucepans, you may stay."

So she stayed there, and washed the pots and scraped the saucepans, and did all the dirty work. And since she gave no name, they called her Cap o'Rushes.

Time went on, and one day there was to be a great ball in the neighborhood, and the servants were allowed to go and look at the grand people. Cap o'Rushes said she was too tired to go with them, and stayed at home.

But as soon as they were all gone, she took off her cloak of rushes and washed herself and combed her hair and went to the ball. And there was no lady there who looked so fine or danced so well. Her master's son was there, and from the moment he saw her, he had eyes for no one else. When he danced with her, he asked her name and where she came from, but she would not say. And before the ball was over, she slipped away home; and when the other servants returned, she seemed to be asleep.

Next morning they said to her, "You did miss a sight last night, Cap o'Rushes."

"What was that?" said she.

"Why, the prettiest young lady you ever saw. The young master never took his eyes off her."

"I should have liked to have seen that," said Cap o'Rushes.

"Well," said they, "there's to be another dance this evening, and perhaps she'll be there."

But when evening came, Cap o'Rushes said she was too worn out from her work to go with them. However, as soon as they were out of the house she pulled off her rushen cloak, washed herself, and away she went to the ball. The master's son was very joyful to see her, and would not dance with anyone else. Again he tried to discover her name and where she came from, but in vain. And before the ball was over she slipped away home; and when the other maids came back, there she was in bed, pretending to be asleep.

Next day they said to her again, "Oh, Cap o'Rushes, you should have been at the ball last night. The pretty

lady was there again, and the young master would dance with no one else all evening."

"I should have liked to have seen that," she said.

"Well," said they, "there's to be another ball to-night, and you must come with us."

But when the evening came Cap o'Rushes said she was too tired, and though the others urged her, she would stay at home. As soon as they were gone she took off her rushen cloak, washed herself, and ran off to the ball. The master's son was very glad when he saw her, and would not leave her side all evening. He swore that he must know her name and where she lived, yet she still would not tell. When the time came for her to go, he gave her a ring, and said that if he did not see her again, he would die. Yet while he was not looking she slipped away, and was in bed with her eyes shut by the time the other maids came home.

The next day they said to her, "Oh, Cap o'Rushes, what a pity you did not come last night to see the pretty lady, for there's no more dances."

"Aye, I should like to have seen her," said she.

Now the master's son tried every way he knew of to find out who the lady was that he had danced with, or where she lived, but no matter whom he asked, he could discover nothing. He grew ill and worn from longing, till he had to take to his bed.

"Make some gruel for the young master," said the mistress to the cook, "for he's sick to death for love of the pretty lady he danced with at the ball." So the cook set about making it, when Cap o'Rushes came in.

"What are you doing?" said she.

"I'm making some gruel for the young master," said the cook.

"Let me make it," said Cap o'Rushes.

Well, the cook said no at first, but at last she said yes, and Cap o'Rushes made the gruel. And when it was done, she slipped the ring into it when no one was looking, and the cook carried it upstairs. The master's son drank it, and found his ring at the bottom.

"Send for the cook!" cried he. So up she came.

"Who made this gruel?" he asked.

"I did," said the cook, frightened.

"No you didn't," said the young man, looking at her. "Tell me who did it, and I won't hurt you."

"Well, then, it was the new kitchen maid."

"Send her to me," said the master's son. So the cook went down, and up came Cap o'Rushes.

"Did you make this gruel?" said he.

"Yes, I did," said she.

"Where did you get this ring?" said he.

"From him that gave it to me," said Cap o'Rushes.

"Who are you, then?" cried he.

"I'll show you," said she. And she pulled off her cloak of rushes, and there she was in her fine dress.

Now the master's son was cured of his sickness at once, and though Cap o'Rushes still would not say who she was or where she came from, nothing would do for him but that they should be married as soon as may be. It was to be a very grand wedding, and all the neighbors were asked from miles around. Cap o'Rushes' father was to be one of the guests.

Before the wedding she went to the cook. "I want you to make all the meat without a bit of salt," said she.

"That'll be very nasty," said the cook.

"Never mind," said she, "but do as I say."

"Very well," said the cook.

So the wedding day came, and Cap o'Rushes and the master's son were married. After they came back from church, all the company sat down to dinner. But when the meat came on, it was so tasteless they could not eat it. Cap o'Rushes' father tried first one dish and then another, and at last he burst out crying.

"What's the matter?" asked the master's son.

"Oh," said he. "Once I had a dear daughter. I asked her how much she loved me, and she said 'As much as fresh meat loves salt.' And I was angry, and drove her out of the house, for I thought she cared nothing for me.

And now I see she loved me best of all. And she may be dead for aught I know."

"No, Father, here she is," said Cap o'Rushes. And she went up to him and put her arms round him.

And so they were all happy ever after.

This English variant of "Cinderella" is believed to be one of the sources of **King Lear**. *The story is very old, and known in many European countries.*

GONE IS GONE

In the north country, where grass grows on the roofs of the cottages, there once lived a farmer who was not pleased with his lot in life. "I do more work in a day than you do in three," he said to his wife almost every noontime and evening when he came in from the fields. "I toil and sweat, plowing and sowing and harvesting, while you laze around the house."

At last his wife grew tired of hearing this talk. "Very well, husband," she said. "Tomorrow I will do your work, and you can do mine. I'll go out to cut the hay, and you can stay here and keep the house." "Good," the husband said, and he laughed to himself, thinking how easy it would be.

So the next morning the wife put the scythe over her shoulder and went out into the fields. Her husband thought that he would begin by churning the cream, so there would be butter for the porridge at dinner. He churned and he churned, yet the butter did not come. "This is hot work," he said, and he went out the cottage door and down into the cellar to get some ale.

But just as he turned the tap on the barrel, he heard a noise overhead, which was the pig coming into the cottage, because he had left the door open. He ran up the cellar steps as fast as he could, but he was too late. The pig had already knocked over the churn, and was rooting and grunting in it. The husband shouted and ran at the pig, and booted him out the door. Then he turned and looked at the churn lying on its side with the cream spilt over the floor.

"Well," he said. "Gone is gone."

Then he remembered the ale, and ran back down to the cellar. But he had left the tap open, and all the ale had run out of the barrel, so that there was none left to drink.

"Well, gone is gone," he said again.

Now the husband thought that he would grind some oatmeal for the porridge. But while he was doing this he heard the cow mooing in the barn, and remembered that she was still shut up in her stall and had had nothing to eat all morning. As he hurried to let her out, he saw that the sun was already high in the sky. He thought that it was too late and too far to lead the cow down to the meadow, and that instead he would cut her some grass from the cottage roof, for a fine crop was growing there.

Then he said to himself that it would be much easier if he could only get the cow herself onto the roof. So he laid a plank across from the hill at the back of the cottage, and fetched her out of her stall. She didn't want to go onto the roof very much; but he pulled and coaxed and at last got her over. Then he thought he had better tie her up, so she wouldn't fall off. So he fastened a rope to her halter, and put the other end down the chimney.

He climbed down off the roof and hurried back into the cottage. It was full of chickens, for he had left the door open again, and they had got into the oats. He shouted and ran at the chickens, and shooed them out the door. Then he turned and looked at the bowl knocked over, and all the oatmeal that he had ground scattered over the floor.

"Well," he said. "Gone is gone."

He took the end of the cow's rope that was hanging down the chimney and tied it around his leg. Then he filled the big iron kettle with water and hung it over the fire, for it was dinnertime; and as fast as he could he ground more oats. The water began to boil, and he put them in. But while he was doing this, the cow fell off the roof, and as she fell she dragged the husband up the chimney by his leg. There he stuck fast, shouting and

cursing; and as for the cow, she hung halfway down the wall outside.

It was now long past noon, and the wife, who had been cutting hay all morning, grew tired of waiting for her husband to call her home to dinner and started back to the cottage. As she came up the hill the first thing she saw was the cow hanging from the roof. She ran up and cut the rope with her scythe, and the cow fell to the ground. At the same time, inside, down fell her husband headfirst into the kettle of porridge.

The wife heard the noise and ran into the cottage. There was spilt cream and oats everywhere, and a smell of ale from the cellar, and her husband upside down in the kettle. She pulled him out, and there he stood on the floor dripping porridge.

"Well, husband," said she. "Gone is gone. From today forth, you do your work, and I'll do mine, and we'll say no more about it."

The story of the husband and wife who exchange roles is known throughout Europe; this version is Scandinavian. In certain villages in Greece, I have been told, men and women actually do trade roles one day of each year. The men put on their wives' clothes, tend the house and children, and go to church; while the women dress as men, work at their husbands' jobs, and sit in the cafés.

MOTHER HOLLE

ONCE upon a time there was a widower who had a daughter named Rosa, and when his wife had been dead some years he married a widow who had a little girl of her own. Now the new wife was much fonder of her own child. She fed her with the richest food, gave her fine clothes to wear, and let her lie idle all day. But Rosa had to eat scraps and wear rags and do all the work of the house; and if she were slow about it her stepmother beat her.

One winter day Rosa was sitting by the well spinning, when she cut her finger. As she leaned over to wash the blood off the spindle, it slipped from her hands and dropped into the water. She ran back to the house and told what had happened. Her stepmother scolded her mercilessly.

"You stupid girl!" she shouted. "You lost the

spindle; well, now you'd just better go find it."

The poor girl went back to the well crying, not knowing what to do. She was afraid to go home without the spindle, but how ever was she to get it? At last she grew so desperate that she jumped into the well.

When she came to herself again, she was lying in a warm beautiful meadow. There was no sun in the sky, but the air was full of light, and there were flowers everywhere.

Rosa started walking across the meadow, and presently she came to an apple tree, its branches bent down with ripe fruit. It called out to her: "Oh, shake me, shake me! All my apples are ripe!" So Rosa shook the tree until all the apples had fallen. She took one to eat, piled the rest up, and went on.

Next she saw a cow grazing. It mooed at her: "Oh, milk me, milk me! My bag is heavy!" So Rosa sat down and milked the cow into a pail. She had a drink of milk, and went on.

Soon she came to a baker's oven. It called out to her, "Oh, open me, open me! My bread is burning!" So Rosa opened the oven and pulled out all the loaves. She took one, set the rest aside to cool, and went on.

At last she saw a little house. At the window was an old woman, who looked so strange and fierce that Rosa was frightened and wanted to run away. But the old woman said, "Don't be afraid, dear child. I am Mother Holle. Come, stay with me, and help with my housework."

The old woman spoke so kindly that Rosa took courage and agreed to work for her. "Very good," said Mother Holle. "You must keep the house clean, and take care to make my bed nicely and shake it up till the feathers fly, so that it may snow on earth. If you serve me well, you won't regret it."

So Rosa came to live with Mother Holle. She worked hard, and always shook the bed so that the feathers flew about like snowflakes. Mother Holle treated her well, and every day there was boiled meat or roast meat for dinner.

But after she had been there some time, Rosa grew sad. Though she was a thousand times better off than she had been before, she longed to go home and see her father again. At last she said to Mother Holle, "You have been very good to me, but I am homesick. I must go back to my father."

"Very well," said Mother Holle. "It is right that you should do that. I'll send you back myself." She gave Rosa the spindle she had lost; then she took her by the hand and led her to a door that had never been opened before. As Rosa passed through, gold came raining down from above and clung to her, so that she was covered

with it from head to toe. "That's your reward for serving me as you have done," said Mother Holle. She shut the door, and Rosa found herself in the world again, not far from her father's house.

When she came into the yard, the rooster was perched on the edge of the well, and he crowed:

"Cock-a-doodle-doo,
Our golden girl is home anew."

When Rosa went into the house her father embraced her and wept tears of joy, for he had thought her dead. The stepmother was not so happy to see her, but she made a great fuss over her because she was covered with gold.

Rosa told them all that had happened, and when her stepmother heard the story she wanted the same fortune for her own fat lazy daughter. So she told her to go sit by the well and spin. The lazy girl pricked her finger on a bramblebush to make it bloody, and then she threw the spindle into the well and jumped after it.

She woke up in the same beautiful meadow as her sister, and walked the same way. Presently she came to the apple tree, and it began to cry out, "Oh, shake me, shake me! All of my apples are ripe!"

"Why should I?" said the girl. "At home I don't eat common apples; I have oranges and grapes."

She walked on, and soon she came to the cow. "Oh, milk me, milk me!" it mooed. "My bag is heavy!"

"Why should I?" said the lazy daughter. "At home I don't drink milk; I have wine and beer."

She went on, and came to the baker's oven, and it called out, "Oh, open me, open me! My bread is burning!"

"Why should I?" said the girl. "At home I don't eat bread; I have cake and white rolls."

Soon she came to Mother Holle's house. She was not afraid of her looks, and agreed to work for her at once.

On the first day the lazy girl tried to do as Mother Holle told her, for she wanted the reward. But she was not used to hard labor, and knew nothing about housework, so she did everything wrong. The second day she began to take it easy, and when Mother Holle scolded her she grew sulky. On the third day she was so cross and tired that she didn't even want to get up in the morning. She cleaned the house very badly, and when she made Mother Holle's bed she didn't shake it up properly, so that no snow fell on earth and the fields were grey and bare.

Mother Holle soon had enough of the lazy girl, and told her to go home. The girl was glad, for she thought that now she too would be covered with gold. Mother

Holle gave her back her spindle, and took her to the door. But as the girl passed through, instead of gold, there was a rain of tar. "That's your reward for serving me as you have done," said Mother Holle, and she shut the door, and the girl found herself in the world again, near her home.

As she came into the yard, the rooster on the edge of the well crowed:

"Cock-a-doodle-doo,
Our dirty girl is home anew."

When the lazy girl's mother saw her, she screamed and scolded. Then she got hot water and scrubbing brushes. But the pitch refused to come off—it stuck to the girl as long as she lived.

This tale from the Grimm Brothers has parallels in many European countries. Mother Holle is probably related to the old German goddess Holde, patroness of spinning and wells, who also had powers over the weather.

TOMLIN

IN Scotland there was once a forest called Carter-haugh Wood. The trees grew taller there, and the grass thicker, and in the midst of the wood was a green glade and a well grown round with roses. Yet few men would go near it, for fear of meeting one of the fairy people, who demanded a forfeit from all who passed that way. From some they took gold or silver; from others their clothes and jewels; and if a young maid went into the wood, it was said, they would take her maidenhood.

Now near Carterhaugh Wood there was a castle, and one of the daughters of its lord was called Janet. She was proud and daring, and cared little for such tales. So one summer's day she braided up her long hair and tucked up her long gown, and ran off to the wood.

She walked on and on through it, and met no one, until she came to the well. There she saw the roses

growing, fairer than any in her father's garden. She bent
to pluck one, but she had hardly broken the stem when
up started the elf-knight Tomlin, crying:

> "Why pullest thou the rose, Lady,
> And why breaks thou the wand?
> Or why comes thou to Carterhaugh
> Withouten my command?"

But Janet stood her ground, and said that Carterhaugh Wood was her father's, and had been her father's
father's, and that she would come and go there as she
pleased, without asking leave of him or any man. Then
Tomlin laughed, and said that he was no man, yet his
claim was older than hers, and she must pay forfeit to
him. He put his arms around Janet and kissed her, and
laid her on the grass, and she did not say him nay.

Summer passed, and autumn too; the leaves fell
from the trees, and Janet was with child. Her father saw
how it was with her, and asked to know which of his
knights was to blame, so that they might be married. But
Janet answered him:

> "If that I go with child, father,
> Myself must bear the blame;
> There's not a lord about your hall
> Shall give my babe his name."

Then she braided up her hair and tucked up her gown and ran off to Carterhaugh Wood. She came to the well and plucked a rose, and up started Tomlin. Janet told him what had passed between her and her father, and that he wished to marry her to one of his knights.

"I was a human knight once," said Tomlin. "But long years ago, when I was riding back from the hunt on a cold and windy evening, I took the shorter way through Carterhaugh Wood. The Queen of Elfland saw me and cast her spell over me, so that I fell from my horse in a swoon. And when I woke again, I was with her in her land. Very pleasant it is there; yet if I were a man again, I would marry you."

And was there no way that could be? said Janet. Yes, there was one way, said Tomlin, but it was hard. That very night was Halloween, when all the fairy folk would ride across the country; and if Janet would hide herself at midnight by Miles Cross where the roads meet, she might see him pass.

"But how shall I know you, Tomlin," asked Janet, "among so many strange knights that I never saw before?"

"Thus," said Tomlin. "You will see a troop of riders all on black horses, and then a troop on brown; and you must let them both pass you by. But the third troop will be mounted on all milk-white steeds. The Queen of Elf-land will ride among them, and I at her side, with one hand gloved and one hand bare. When you see me you must run to my horse's head, seize its bridle, and pull me down. Dare you do this?"

"Aye," said Janet.

"But you must do more," said Tomlin. "When I am off my horse, you must hold me fast in your arms, what-ever may come. For the fairy folk will try all their spells on me, and change me into many strange and dreadful shapes; yet you must hold me fast and fear me not. Dare you do this?"

"Aye," said Janet.

"But you must do more," said Tomlin. "For at the last, they will change me into a burning branch, and then you must cast me into the water beside Miles Cross, and I will become a naked man again. Then you must wrap your cloak around me, and cover me out of sight. Dare you do this?"

"Aye," said Janet.

So the day passed, and the night came on dark and eerie. In the village and the castle they barred the shutters and sat by the fires. And Janet braided up her hair and tucked up her gown, and went out from the castle, and hid herself by Miles Cross.

Presently the dark grew thicker, and the wind blew stronger, and the fairy hunt came riding by. First came a troop on black horses, and then a troop on brown. And the third troop was all on milk-white steeds; and among them rode the Queen of Elfland, and by her side an armored knight with one hand gloved and one hand bare.

Then Janet ran out and seized the horse's bridle, and pulled its rider down. And all the rest of the hunt came round them, shrieking and howling.

As Janet held Tomlin fast in her arms, they turned him into a bear, huge and hairy. Yet she held on. Then the bear became a hawk, fierce and wild; yet she held on. Then the hawk became a wolf, grey and grim and snarling; yet she held on. Then the wolf became a snake, hissing and coiling; yet she held on. Then the snake became a block of frozen ice; yet Janet held on still.

Then at last the block of ice became a burning branch. Janet flung it into the water, and Tomlin was restored to his human shape, naked as the day he was born. She wrapped her cloak around him, and the spell was broken.

A great sigh went up from the court of Elfland, and the queen cried out:

"Had I but known, Tomlin, Tomlin,
A lady would ransom thee,
I'd have taken out thy two grey eyes,
Put in two eyes of tree.

Had I but known, Tomlin, Tomlin,
Before we came from home,
I'd have taken out thy heart of flesh,
Put in a heart of stone."

Then she and all the hunt turned and rode off into the night.

This Scottish tale of true love, originally a ballad, dates back at least to the mid-sixteenth century, and has parallels in Greek myth. The "wild hunt" of witches, goblins, and fairy folk is still believed to ride over the countryside on certain nights of the year in many parts of Europe.

SOURCES
OF THE TALES

CLEVER GRETCHEN. Based on "The Skillful Huntsman" from *Pepper and Salt* by Howard Pyle, New York, 1885.

MANKA AND THE JUDGE. Based on "The Wise Little Girl" from *Russian Fairy Tales* by Aleksandr Afanas'ev, New York, 1945, and "The Peasant's Clever Daughter" from *Household Tales* by Jacob and Wilhelm Grimm, London, 1884.

THE BLACK GEESE. Based partly on "The Magic Swan–Geese" from *Russian Fairy Tales* by Aleksandr Afanas'ev, New York, 1945.

MIZILCA. Based on "Mizilca" from *European Folk Ballads*, edited by Erich Seeman, Copenhagen, 1967.

THE BAKER'S DAUGHTER. Based on "The Owl Was a Baker's Daughter" from *Nursery Rhymes and Nursery Tales* by J.O. Halliwell, London 1843.

THE MASTERMAID. Based on "The Mastermaid" from *Popular Tales from the Norse* by Peter C. Asbjörnsen and Jorgen E. Moe, translated by George Dasent, Edinburgh, 1888.

· *Sources of the Tales* ·

MOLLY WHUPPIE. Based on "Molly Whuppie" from *Folk-Lore,* Vol. II, 1891.

THE HAND OF GLORY. Based on "The Servant Maid of High Spittal" from *Notes on the Folk-lore of the Northern Counties of England and the Borders* by William Henderson, London, 1866.

MAID MALEEN. Based on "Maid Maleen" from *Household Tales* by Jacob and Wilhelm Grimm, London, 1884.

KATE CRACKERNUTS. Based on "The Story of Kate Crackernuts" from *Folk-Lore,* Vol. I, 1890.

THE SLEEPING PRINCE. Based on the title story from *Incarnat, Blanc et Or* by Paul Delarue, Paris, 1955. (Translated from "El Rey durmiente en su lecho" in *Cuentos populares recogidos en Estremadura* by Sergio Hernandez de Soto, Madrid, 1886.)

CAP o'RUSHES. Based on "Cap o'Rushes" from *Folk-Lore,* Vol. I, 1890.

GONE IS GONE. Based on "The Husband Who Was to Mind the House" from *Popular Tales from the Norse* by Peter C. Asbjörnsen and Jorgen E. Moe, translated by George Dasent, Edinburgh, 1888.

MOTHER HOLLE. Based on "Mother Holle" from *Household Tales* by Jacob and Wilhelm Grimm, London, 1884.

TOMLIN. Based on "Tam Lin" from *English and Scottish Popular Ballads* by Francis James Child, London, 1882–98.

ABOUT THE AUTHOR

ALISON LURIE has read and loved children's books all her life. Many of the famous children's classics, she believes, "are, or were when they first appeared, deeply subversive. That is, they dealt with matters that were denied in adult life and/or literature, or they mocked ideals and institutions that were commonly regarded with solemn approval."

Ms. Lurie is the author of six highly regarded novels, including *The Nowhere City*, *The War Between the Tates*, and *Only Children*. She is a regular contributor to *The New York Review of Books*, and to *Ms.*, *Harper's*, and *The New York Times Book Review*.

A professor of English and children's literature at Cornell University, she is co-editor of the Garland series, Classics of Children's Literature, 1621–1932, and a member of the board of the magazine, *Children's Literature*. *Clever Gretchen* is her first book for young people.

ABOUT THE ILLUSTRATOR

MARGOT TOMES's delightful and distinctive pictures have appeared in more than thirty books for children, including *Little Sister and the Month Brothers*, *Jorinda and Joringel*, and *The Sorcerer's Apprentice*. A graduate of Pratt Institute, Ms. Tomes lives and works in New York City.